HACKED!

D0167092

NANOVOR™

HACKED!

written by Mur Lafferty and Ryan Payne
created by Jordan Weisman

RP|KIDS
PHILADEPHIA • LONDON

©2009 by Smith and Tinker, Inc.

Printed in The United States of America

9   8   7   6   5   4   3   2   1
Digit on the right indicates the number of this printing

Library of Congress Control Number: 2009932169
ISBN 978-0-7624-3756-6

Inks by Jon Alderink
Colors by Shane Small
Cover and interior design by Ryan Hayes
Edited by Jenny Scott Tynes
Typography: Eurostile & Rexlia

Running Press Book Publishers
2300 Chestnut Street
Philadelphia, PA 19103-4371

Visit us on the web!
www.runningpress.com
www.nanovor.com
www.hanoverhigh.com

Secrets

From "Everywhere Fast," Lucas Nelson's Journal

When I was a kid, secrets were nothing more than a way to stay out of trouble or show your best friend that you had her back. Now, they're something more. And I have some big ones.

When I write my memoirs—I guess I'll wait till I'm rich and old, like thirty-five—I'm sure I'll say things like how I discovered the nanosphere and the little critters living in it on purpose.

But the truth is, I never set out to discover nanovor.

I was just doing a report on dust mites—those little monsters that live on us and eat our dead skin like potato chips or something—and while looking through one of Doc Zap's high-powered microscopes, I wondered if other little monsters lived anywhere else. We've always dreamed of things living on the Internet—we just always thought they'd be AI (Artificial Intelligence).

So I kludged together the very first nanoscope: a primitive abacus compared to the radically slick toys that Doc Zap made for us soon after. But it did what I needed it to do, mainly take a peek inside my computer at the microscopic level.

What I saw were these little creatures living in the computers! Nanovor!

Or rather, nanoscopic creatures. Super ultra mega small. We haven't figured out much about them except that they live their happy, violent little lives inside computer chips—any computer chips—and they're old. Super ultra mega old. There are hundreds of different kinds, maybe thousands. We're not sure yet.

They live to fight! As soon as we figured that out, we realized it wasn't a big step to collect them and fight them. It's really fun. And almost everyone thinks it's just a game.

Doc Zap wants it that way. Right now, it's only me, my best friend, Drew, some other friends, and Doc Zap who know the truth.

Oh, and some upperclassmen. Okay, and there's crazy Dr. Diamondback. He's like a disgraced unemployed doctor from S.K.Y. Lab Technologies, and he'd just love to get control of the nanovor to, well, I'm sure he has some plan. For that matter, I don't think we'd want S.K.Y. Labs involved either. The way Doc Zap talks about them, they're the evilest of the evil megacorps.

You wanna know what gets me about this whole thing? I discover these nanovor and their home in the nanosphere, and I invent the nanoscope, which is what we use to watch and control them, and Doc Zap wants me to come up with something ELSE for the Emerald City Science Fair! I'm only a freshman—haven't I accomplished enough this year? I discover a new life-form that's not even carbon based, and he wants me to cure cancer and build a better Web browser at the same time.

But I think I might actually have something that'll impress even Doc Zap. If I can just get it done on time. Kids don't really need sleep, do they?

So I need to stop writing and get back to working on that. And by the way, keep an eye on the T-shirts I'm wearing—I've hidden a secret phrase in them. If you find it, write it down below, and go to **www.hanoverhigh.com/hacked** and enter it there. I'll give you a small gift if you can figure it out!

~Lucas Out

ucas Nelson pushed through the doors of Hanover High right at lunchtime on Thursday. In one hand he clutched a sweaty note from his mother, hoping the school would excuse his tardiness, and in the other he cradled a cardboard box containing circuit boards sandwiched between pieces of black egg-crate foam. He was nearly there; after he installed these boards, he'd need only a few more components for his science-fair project.

As he stepped away from the doors, a hand reached under his box to tickle him in the ribs.

"Hey!" he shouted, nearly dropping the box and stumbling back over his feet.

One strong hand grabbed his free hand, another steadied the box so he wouldn't drop it. Lucas blinked and saw the brilliant smile of Drew, his best friend.

"Gotcha," she said.

"Not funny," he said, rearranging his box so it was safer in his arms. He glanced down the hall to check for Principal Sturn and headed away from the office.

Her smile vanished, and her eyes widened in her patented curious-Drew look as she took in what he was carrying. "More science-fair secrecy?"

Lucas nodded. The Emerald City Science Fair invited schools from several cities in their region to compete. The panel of expert judges was impressive, including professors from the local state university as well as prominent companies, such as S.K.Y. Lab Technologies. Winners received trophies, small scholarships, and the right to go on to a state competition.

"I'm telling you, Drew, Doc Zap isn't going to stop hounding me until I'm dead. Last night I was up tearing apart half the devices in my house to get the components for these boards. If I win, hopefully my Mom won't kill me when she finds out what I did to her cell phone. I was hoping to get here before lunch, but it looks like we're halfway through."

Drew pulled her backpack around and pushed aside the

black nanoscope to open a zippered pocket. She pulled out a thin, flat bar and handed it to Lucas. "Here. This should help."

He grimaced and tried to pass it off as a smile when he accepted it. Drew played soccer and volleyball and ran track, so she always had some sort of flat, dense, tasteless protein-delivery bar. Lucas realized he didn't have an argument against eating it, and he was hungry. He tore off the silver wrapper and took a bite of the chalky, vaguely vanilla food product. "Thanks."

"Did ah missh anyfing good 'ooday?" he asked through a mouthful of dense goo.

She shrugged. "Same old. The Snake Pit is offering to take on all challengers at lunch. Of course, Bulk Damage looks like he'll put you through a wall if you dare to even consider beating him."

Lucas, Drew, and their friends who knew the truth about nanovor called themselves the "Lab Rats." Their chief rivals, the "Snake Pit," also knew the truth. Made up of upperclassmen bullies, including Sam "Bulk Damage" Bramage, the Snake Pit had claimed the nanovor competition as their own and made themselves the team to beat. The group was led by the scheming Ben Arneson, shrewd wide receiver for the Hanover High football team and also included pudgy Jacob Edison, the school's former alpha geek until Lucas arrived last fall.

Lucas swallowed his mouthful slowly; the protein bar was not the only thing that was difficult to ingest. The Snake Pit had their own nanoscopes, secret technology perfected by Mr. Sapphire the science teacher (or, as he was called by the Lab Rats, "Doc Zap"), that they had stolen from Lucas. He'd been the victim, but he couldn't help feeling a little responsible, like there was something more he could have done to stop them.

"Is Dana going to be there?" Lucas sheepishly asked.

Drew sighed loudly. "Lucas, if you mess around with Dana Diamondback, don't be surprised if you get snake bit. She's head of the cheer squad, she's dating Ben Arneson, and she's Dr. Diamondback's daughter. What about those three things doesn't scream, 'DANGER, WILL ROBINSON?'" She waved her arms around, robot style, till Lucas laughed.

He shook his head. "Look, she's always nice to me. And I think people underestimate her. She's pretty smart."

Drew put her hands on her trim hips. "Yeah. That's why you like her. She's smart."

She tapped Lucas's cardboard box with her knuckles. "Speaking of smart, are you going to make it?"

They climbed the stairs to the second floor to Doc Zap's office. "I think so," said Lucas. "It'll be close, but these subsystems are all done. I just need to cobble together the final boards to finish."

"Can we watch you test it?" came a voice from a doorway. They both turned to face Nathan, their junior-class friend. He exited the room and snaked his arm around Drew to squeeze briefly, then let her go.

"Not sure," Lucas said, not looking at their small hug. "I think I want to test it on my own to make sure it doesn't . . . you know . . . ."

Drew laughed loudly. "Call up Blizzard and sign us all up for fifteen World of Warcraft accounts?"

Lucas ignored her laughter. "Something like that, yeah. So what's up, Nathan?"

Nathan grinned. He had a wide, smile that caused most of those around him to reflect it, Lucas and Drew included. "I've been looking for you two. There's something you need to see." He led them down the hall. Drew shrugged at Lucas and followed.

Nathan was one of the popular kids in school. He was a drama star, good-looking, friendly, and welcome in any club or group—including the Snake Pit. Lucas had always wondered how Drew could rag him for talking to Dana and not bother Nathan for hanging out with the same group Dana did.

A shout came from the Technology Lab, where students were gathered around the door, straining to see in.

"Is this the 'taking all challengers' thing the Snake Pit is doing?" asked Lucas, trying to peek through. He spotted an image projected onto the wall but couldn't tell what it was. He could guess though. Ben—or, more likely, Jacob—had rigged the nanoscopes to project the battles so everyone could view them. Smart, he grudgingly admitted; now nano-vor battles were a spectator sport, with people cheering on their favorites. Trash talk was high, mostly among students who had their own nanoscopes linked together, battling.

"We'll never get in there," Drew said.

"Oh ye of little faith," said Nathan. He cleared his throat and took a breath. Lucas had seen him do the same thing before delivering a monologue onstage. "Principal Sturn, you look stunning in your new suit!"

Lucas had a momentary fear that someone had invented

a teleportation device for the science fair, as most of the students had vanished in a flurry. Then he realized what Nathan had said and grinned in admiration of the upperclassman.

"After you," Nathan said with a flourish, ushering Drew and Lucas into the now mostly empty room.

Dana Diamondback focused on the Snake Pit as they battled, frowning at their unfocused fighting style.

Ben, Jacob, and Bulk were all working to beat their opponent, another upperclassman by the name of Fred, but they didn't even attempt to unite to take him down before they turned on each other. Right as Ben's Tank Walker was about to finish off Fred's school-bus-looking Electropod, Jacob's Giga Tangler sideswiped the Tank Walker with a Whirlwind attack, throwing it out of the game.

Dana shook her head. They still needed discipline.

A ripple of fear went through the crowd then, and most of the kids made "Gotta get to class" noises, dashing out the door. Dana narrowed her eyes.

Drew Ettelson walked into the room looking apologetic

and ridiculous. That girl was always worried about breaking the rules.

As if to prove Dana correct, Drew said, "Clever, if unfair."

She spoke to Nathan, who walked in behind her, grinning his "You have to forgive me—I'm a nice guy" smile.

Nathan shrugged. "They needed to get to class anyway. People have been tardy all day."

If Nathan and Drew were here, that meant—yes, there he was. The smartest kid in school, Lucas Nelson, held a cardboard box as tenderly as he would hold a collection of human souls.

The battle on the wall had completely entranced Drew and Lucas. The four battling upperclassmen and Dana studied their linked nanoscopes intently a couple of feet away, but they may as well have been statues.

After Bulk's nanovor destroyed Fred's final nanovor, Lucas glanced over at them. Dana caught his eyes and smiled, lifting her hand in a little wave. Lucas blushed as he waved back, then turned back to watch the battle. Only two nanovor were left: Bulk's Electrobull and an armored Gamma Fury.

Ben controlled the Gamma Fury. Often, people chose

nanovor that were quite like themselves, and this situation was no different. Quick, wily, and dangerous, just like the senior who controlled it, the Gamma Fury danced around the still Electrobull, which waited.

Speaking of people who were like their nanovor, you'd have to be dumber than Sam "Bulk Damage" Bramage not to know he controlled the Electrobull, which was about as subtle as a brick through a computer monitor. The big, stupid, strong guy controlled the big, stupid, strong nanovor. Dana knew that head to head, the 'bull could totally destroy the Fury. But they weren't going head-to-head. They were controlled, and the Gamma Fury's controller had a brain, while the Electrobull's didn't.

Dana watched as Bulk Damage bellowed his fury and made his Electrobull charge. The Gamma Fury simply danced out of the way and attacked the big tank from behind with a mighty Thunder Flash. Weakened from earlier battles, the Electrobull stiffened and collapsed in a puddle of goo. The strategy that Dana had whispered to Ben two minutes earlier paid off, and the victor pumped his fist in the air. Dana sat back, pleased.

Grinning, Ben faced his red-faced foe. The only person

Bulk Damage wouldn't hit was Ben, so Ben could say whatever he liked. "Buddy, I'm telling you, if you aren't going to choose nanovor that think for themselves, you have to think for them."

Bulk cracked his broad jaw to speak, but Ben interrupted him. "And Lucas!" he said, hopping up from his chair and nearly crashing into Dana. She glared at his back but smoothed her features as Lucas looked over toward them again, his tired-looking eyes slitted in suspicion. "Just the man I wanted to see! You wouldn't be up for a friendly bout, would you? I've got some new moves I'd love to show you."

Lucas glanced at the clock. Dana knew he didn't like to back down from a challenge from Ben—especially with her there. But he had Drew with him, and she was the irritating voice of reason whenever Lucas wanted to do something fun.

"Lucas, we need to get to class soon," Drew said.

Lucas didn't look at her. His eyes flickered to Dana and then back to Ben. He gave a short nod. "Okay."

Drew rolled her eyes and groaned.

Lucas selected his swarm of nanovor, and the three appeared in the projected image on the wall. Storm Spinner, Storm Hunter, and Circuit Tank. Dana frowned slightly.

Ben's preferred nanovor were Gamma Fury, Spike Spine, and the bulky Tank Walker. Lucas would have some problems, it looked like. His Storm Spinner and Storm Hunter were both Velocitron nanovor, fast and powerful but often weak against the heavily armored Magnamods, which is what Ben's Gamma Fury and Tank Walker were. Dana guessed Lucas's hope lay with his Circuit Tank, an armored Magnamod.

Lucas urged his Storm Spinner, a flashy silver quadruped with a wicked blade on its face, into the nanosphere to meet Ben's Gamma Fury. The Gamma Fury advanced, and the Storm Spinner threw a Crystal Trap at it, stopping it in its tracks. Lucas pushed his nanovor forward for a physical attack, sacrificing it in order to hopefully do a bit of damage before it exploded in a gush of silver.

And with a sizzle and a squelch the Storm Spinner was history and the Gamma Fury was free of its prison. Dana wasn't sure if that was the wisest of sacrifices, but she was always looking to see what she could learn from other nanovor players.

Lucas sent in his Circuit Tank, a nanovor that looked like a cross between a grasshopper and a crab. Dana's eyes fell on the box at Lucas's feet and then on Nathan, who was standing next to the seated Drew, cheering on Lucas.

Dana slid out of her chair and sidled over to Nathan as Lucas had his Circuit Tank hit Ben's Gamma Fury with its Flamethrower attack. Gamma Fury crumpled into an ashy heap and disappeared.

Nathan didn't notice her until she bumped his elbow with hers, nonchalantly watching the battle. Lucas had pulled his Circuit Tank and brought out his Storm Hunter, a graceful, orange, floating nanovor. Ben replaced his defeated Gamma Fury with a thick blue Tank Walker. Dana winced in anticipation; the Tank Walker was a heavily armored Magnamod. What was Lucas thinking?

"Lucas really isn't on his game today, is he?" she asked softly.

Nathan looked down at her, startled. He glanced quickly at Drew, who was immersed in the battle, worry etching lines on her forehead. "He does seem a little off. Why do you ask?" His eyes narrowed.

She shrugged. "Lucas hasn't been around much. Does he have problems at home?"

Nathan shook his head as Lucas's Storm Hunter fixed the Tank Walker with an armor-reducing Stare of Doom. "Oh, no, it's nothing like that. He's just been working on his science project."

Dana nodded and waited for Ben's inevitable Tank Gore assault, which could take out the Storm Hunter in one hit. Nathan winced when it came, and as the room filled with cheers and groans, Dana asked, "So that's what's in the box?"

Nathan nodded absently and watched Lucas's Storm Hunter manage to stay alive for one more attack. "Circuit boards." He let out a held breath as Lucas switched out the Storm Hunter and brought his Circuit Tank back in.

"Really? Is he searching for new nanovor?" Dana asked as the room cheered. The Circuit Tank was faster than Ben's Tank Walker, and it had attacked with a Jump Shot, a fast, armor-ignoring attack. Everyone had expected Lucas to use a Big Power-Up first, but his sudden attack took everyone by surprise. Ben shouted as his Tank Walker disintegrated.

Nathan pumped his fist in the air. "Yeah, Lucas! Where did he learn that trick?" He looked down at Dana's hand on his arm. "Oh, right. No, nothing like new nanovor. Mr. Sapphire won't let Lucas put the nanovor in the science fair. This is something new, something about focusing on someone, hacking mobile devices, accessing private data from the Web. I don't really understand it."

"Wow," Dana said, staring at the wall and not seeing the battling nanovor. Accessing private data from mobile devices? There would be some very prominent scientists judging the science fair, including some of the scientists who had disgraced her father, forcing him to leave his job at S.K.Y. Lab Technologies. This could be useful.

She turned her smile on full force at Nathan. "That's fantastic information, Nathan. Thanks."

Nathan's eyes widened. "Wait a minute, you're not going to mess with him or anything, are you? I mean, Lucas is my friend, and if you mess up his science project—"

Dana patted his arm. "Oh no, I wouldn't dream of messing with his project. I really want him to win, actually. I want this project to be the best it can be. But stick around him, Nathan. I may need you later."

"But, wait, Dana!" Nathan said, but at that point the room erupted into the cheers and jeers of the upperclassmen as Ben's fresh Spike Spine, a Hexite, used a vicious attack and easily defeated the energy-tapped Circuit Tank.

Dana placed her finger over her lips. "Shh. I want to watch the battle." She smiled at his stricken look and went back over to the boys hunched over the nanoscopes.

Lucas was smiling now, closed-mouth and intent. He glanced up once and caught Dana's eye. She smiled at him, and he flushed again, going back to the game. She realized that Ben had played into Lucas's trap as he brought out the final nanovor, his Storm Hunter. Although the Storm Hunter was weakened, so was the Spike Spine, and Velocitrons had the advantage over Hexites.

Two rounds of expertly placed Lotus Cuts had the Storm Hunter victorious over the Spike Spine, with the room cheering loudly and Ben looking stunned.

The bell rang at that moment, and Ben jerked his nanoscope away from the connection with Lucas, who just smiled sheepishly.

"Come on, Dana," Ben said. "We're late for Spanish."

"I'll be along in a minute," she said. "I want to congratulate Lucas."

"Excellent game, Lucas," Dana said as Lucas picked up his belongings.

"Hey, thanks," he said.

"I'd love to hear about your strategy. That was pretty impressive," she said, walking him out of the room. One glance behind her showed Nathan looking worried. She winked at him.

Thursday after school, Lucas was pulling his hair out. He and Drew sat in Mr. Sapphire's—Doc Zap's—science storeroom, taking advantage of the quiet in order for Lucas to finish his science project. The room was actually a long, double-wide hall lined with shelves. Here, Hanover High's science teachers stored their biology and geology samples, microscopes, scales, Bunsen burners, an entire wall of chemicals for in-class experiments, and at least twenty different sizes and styles of test tubes.

Doc Zap allowed Lucas to use the long, narrow worktable stored in the hall. This week, Lucas had his science-fair project spread across the table like a gutted robot from a mad scientist's dream. It was an assortment of circuit boards, scanning devices, and tangled, multicolored wire.

He stepped back from his work, rubbed his eyes, and looked it over from top to bottom, comparing it to the schematics in his notebook.

Lucas twisted his hands in his hair and gave another frustrated yank.

Drew reached out and pulled his hands away. "Stop that," she said.

He let go of his hair. "I just don't know, Drew. How am I going to finish this? There's so much left to do . . . twenty-five."

She stared at him. "Are we giving ourselves number nicknames now? I'd rather be pi, incidentally."

Lucas shook his head as if to clear it. "No, I just decided that I will need twenty-five hours in the day to finish all of this. That's doable, right?"

"Well, we'd need to adjust the rotation of the earth," Drew said. " 'Cause in a month we'd be all turned around if we messed with the clocks."

Lucas quickly did the math in his head and stood up excitedly. "Hey, we'd only have to slow the earth's rotation forty miles per hour. That's not too bad. We can totally do that, right?"

Drew grinned. "Sure, but it sounds like something you'd have time for only after this project is done. Which kind of defeats the whole purpose, right?"

Lucas slumped back on his stool. "Yeah."

Doc Zap's voice floated into the storage room. "Lucas, can you give me a hand in here for a moment?"

"Sure," he said and trudged into Doc Zap's classroom.

Robert "Doc Zap" Sapphire looked up from his work to stare at Lucas blankly. His long gray hair was bound back in a ponytail that Lucas was sure went out of style sometime mid-last-century. He rarely smiled, but Lucas knew his dry, razor wit cut so finely that half his classmates never even knew they'd been cut.

"I'm giving you a hand!" said Lucas.

Doc Zap snorted and returned to his work.

"So what does the nanoscanner need from me?" Lucas asked, looking at Doc Zap's latest project.

The nanoscanner was a device he had built to allow direct access to the nanosphere for Lucas and his friends. Projecting their consciousness through their nanoscopes, they could roam inside the electronic world just like the nanovor.

Doc Zap still wasn't entirely sure whether the nanosphere

was one-hundred percent safe for humans yet, but this hadn't stopped the Lab Rats from venturing in from time to time. They'd found their way into the Internet, found a pretty simple way to bypass the school's secure databases and, of course, seen wild nanovor. Unfortunately, the Snake Pit had also managed to find their way in, much to Lucas's irritation and shame. If he was one of the smartest kids in school, how come he couldn't figure out how to keep Ben Arneson and his idiot friends away from his toys?

"Lucas, if you'd pay attention, we might finish this and you could return to Drew and your project," Doc Zap said. "I need you to hold these two leads, and do not let them touch."

"Sorry Doc. So what are you working on?" Lucas asked, taking the red and green wires from his teacher.

"I've been working on a security system for the nano-scanner, but there is an issue at the nanoscopic level. Your account of Dana Diamondback's problem with the nanovor sensei Spydran got me thinking about how vulnerable we might be to an attack from any of the intelligent nanovor."

Lucas had been worrying about that as well. Most nanovor had very limited intelligence—about that of an average dog. Sometimes, though, an ancient creature collected the intelligence of many nanovor into its own consciousness and gained true sentience. Lucas and his friends had dubbed these "sensei" nanovor, because they also gathered, trained, and fought their own swarms. Lucas had met a friendly sensei, one that seemed interested and patient toward humans.

Spydran was no such sensei.

Spydran saw humans as a plague on the world, and it had found a way to infiltrate and infect Dana's personal home electronics, terrorizing her for weeks.

"So you think you can keep Spydran out of our equipment?" Lucas asked.

"I've been working on a way to keep out everyone we don't want in there."

Meaning the Snake Pit. Lucas and Doc had already talked about the possibility that one of Lucas's friends were talking too much.

Lucas didn't want to believe that, but there was no arguing that Ben Arneson and his friends knew far too much about the nanosphere.

They were getting their information from somewhere.

"And . . . done." Doc stood up and began to adjust the nanoscanner's controls. "All right. You can plug those leads back together."

"That was all you needed?" Lucas frowned, touching the wires together.

"Yes. It was very important, however."

"Oh yeah?" Lucas asked.

"Oh yeah," Doc Zap parroted. "If those leads had touched, you and I could have been pulled into the nanosphere with no hope of escape."

Lucas dropped the wires, now securely fastened benignly. "And you didn't tell me this why?"

Doc Zap smiled slightly. "Where would the fun have been in that? Anyway, it's safe now, but never forget all scientific experimentation comes with risks."

Lucas sputtered but was interrupted by a small freshman girl who appeared in Doc Zap's doorway, out of breath. "Mr. Sapphire? Principal Sturn said to come get you—we had a rotten potato experiment blow up in chemistry. The janitor claims it's a biohazard and won't touch it."

Doc Zap sighed. "Rotten potato is one of the foulest smells that exists. Clever of Mrs. Bindlechner to go home while her kids are studying this fascinating process. I'll be back soon, Lucas. Get to work on your project." He followed the panicky girl down the hall.

Lucas looked once more at the wires that could have caused him to live forever in the nanosphere, then left Doc Zap's classroom to return to Drew.

She had organized the components by kind, size, and color. His notes now had neat checkmarks beside each messy component listing.

"Whoa. What did you do?" he asked, staring at the neat table.

"What you never seem to give yourself time to do," Drew said. "Looks like you have everything. And it looks like you'll have time to build it over the next few days."

Lucas stared at her. "Drew, this is amazing! I—"

A voice from Doc Zap's room interrupted him. "Lucas! Are you back there?"

Drew's look of triumph faded as she recognized the voice.

Lucas turned and yelled back, "Yeah, Dana, we're down here!"

Dana Diamondback came in, all smiles. She wore her cheerleading uniform and looked breathless and tousled as if she had just come from practice. Her eyes widened when she saw the table.

"Wow, you have been busy!" she said.

"Yeah, we still are," Drew said. "Lucas, we should get started putting this together soon. I'm going to need to head home in half an hour, so if you want my help we need to get moving on this."

"Yeah, you're right," Lucas said, watching Dana. She didn't try to touch anything, but she looked closely at each part, ignoring Drew as she moved closer to get a better look at the main circuit board.

"Oh, don't stop on account of me," she said, not looking at them.

"Oh, all right," Lucas said hesitantly. "Drew, I'm going to solder this wire in place if you could hold it."

Drew looked at Dana, who watched them intently, making no sign of leaving, then glanced back at Lucas with an inscrutable look. He shrugged at her.

"You know, I think my mom said to be home around four-thirty, not five," said Drew, "so I'm going to head out. Looks like you have enough help here anyway." She got up, tossed her backpack onto her shoulder, then left without looking back.

Lucas shrugged again. Girls. Who could fathom them? Apparently not even other girls.

"Well, I can help!" Dana said. "What did you need?"

Working on the science project made Lucas relax around Dana at last, and she proved to be a good lab assistant, holding wires steady and helping him assemble and solder.

"That was an amazing win over Ben today, Lucas. I don't know how you did it. It was a brilliant strategy. I thought Ben was going to eat his own nanoscope." She smiled at him, her green eyes shining.

"Oh, uh, thanks," he said, burning his finger with the soldering iron. He stuck his finger in his mouth and blushed.

With Dana helping, the work went quite fast, faster than expected. They managed to make a working prototype in about an hour.

Lucas stretched. "I can't believe we finished it."

Dana studied the unimpressive connected interior of his grand machine. "So what are we building here?" she asked. "If I'm helping, I should know."

"I could tell you, or I could show you." He grinned at her and focused two tiny lenses on her. "Hold still. This won't hurt." He turned it on and stepped back.

She frowned. "What is it doing?"

"Well, right now it's doing facial recognition." He nodded at the monitor, where Dana's face was suddenly displayed. A grid of blue lines followed the contours of her face. It checked the distance between her eyes. Width of her mouth. Cheekbone structure. A dozen other measurements.

"Interesting," Dana said. "And that's what this does?"

"Nope. That's just how it starts out. Needs to know who it's looking at. There, it's got you."

Lucas saw Dana's high-school student-body card on the display, complete with this year's school picture. Then her current class schedule. Her grades.

Near Dana's elbow, a speaker crackled to life.

"Dana Diamondback. Your current grade-point average looks very promising. I see college in your future."

Dana's name sounded very harsh as spoken by the computer-generated voice. Too mechanical. Lucas would have to fix that. But the rest had a great effect on her. She sat back, spine straight, and stared stone-faced at the offending speaker.

"It has access to my file?" She seemed mad, but then her expression changed. "Okay. You've tied it into the school's computer."

"Not quite. In fact, isn't that your MySpace page?"

The monitor now showed the front page of Dana's personal website. It had her picture gallery. Her profile. Then it flashed to a new page and showed a list of her private emails.

"Hey! Lucas! That's private."

"Don't worry. I'm not reading it, and it's not saving any of this. There's no permanent storage."

The speaker crackled again with a burst of static. "After your performance next year at the national cheer-squad competition, you may receive a scholarship offer from Northwest University. But beware! You have not mailed your early application, and the deadline is in two weeks! Beware! Beware!"

"Okay, this is creepy, Lucas. How does it know so much about me?"

Lucas laughed. "It's all right. Really. I call her 'Madame Zeldara.' I'm going to spend the weekend putting a fortune-teller's mask on her to make her all flashy. She shows you how much information you publish about yourself is available. And even things you'd like to keep private aren't very secure."

"My personal information is very secure," Dana said confidently.

Crackle. "You should answer your cell phone," the pile of electronics told her.

Three seconds later, Dana's phone rang.

She jumped and dug her phone out of her pocket. Then laughed.

"All right. I give up. You are going to have to tell me how you did that." But first she did answer her phone. A short conversation that consisted of "Call you back, Ben. Bye."

She hung up immediately. Lucas felt kind of happy that she had hung up on Ben Arneson so quickly.

"It's not so mysterious," he told her, as the speaker crackled out "Beware! Beware!" again. "Besides the facial-recognition software, a scanner reads every electronic device you are carrying. It pulled your cell-phone's information through its Bluetooth chip. The security really isn't very tight. From there it must have picked up your MySpace page. Maybe even your password."

"All right. Sure. My MySpace page and my password are stored on my cell."

"Well, even if they weren't, the system would formulate

hundreds of guesses based on the usual password choices people make. Your birthday. The name of a pet. Any nickname it finds in your phone's text log."

Dana nodded, following along. "And once it had access," she said, "a pattern-recognition program running through my emails or my calendar pulled out data about the cheer competition. And I'm talking with someone about Northwest University. Then you sort that into some basic statements and a couple of high-probability predictions."

Lucas beamed. "You got it."

"Impressive," Dana said. Her eyes were still wide and bright. "What can you do with all of this information?"

"Well, just about anything I want," Lucas admitted. Then he added slyly, "But not what anyone will be expecting."

"That sounds . . . sneaky."

Lucas laughed. "It's not." He turned back to his creation. "Don't sweat it. Once I turn all this off, it retains no memory of anything it's read." He started to disconnect elements one switch at a time. "I'll fix the speaker, make it sound a bit more friendly, and it'll be good to—"

He turned back to Dana. But she was no longer there.

"—go."

To an outsider, Dana supposed the Diamondbacks' basement lab was shining, glorious—the perfect place for a scientist of Dr. Diamondback's caliber to work. And she supposed compared to other labs it was. Well lit, and with an impressive array of computers and large monitors, an electron microscope, a drafting table, and other equipment, it looked state-of-the-art, expensive, and important.

But to her it was but a shell of what the basement once was. Before, it was packed with three times as much equipment. The science equivalent of Home and Garden magazine had once come to photograph it as one of the best private labs in the western hemisphere. It was a lab worthy of her father and his status; he was one of the most important scientists to have ever worked for S.K.Y. Labs Technologies.

Until he'd been forced to resign. Until he'd been let go. But he'd be on top again. If not at S.K.Y. Labs, then somewhere better. Dana was convinced of this.

Dana, now dressed a skirt and a blouse (her dad never took her seriously in her cheerleading uniform), led Ben and Bulk down the stairs to the lab where her dad worked.

She thought about Madame Zeldara and the amazing things Lucas had made her do. Personal data was pretty much close to currency these days, as exhibited by the idiots who put all of their personal data on MySpace and then freaked when someone pointed out that it wasn't private information anymore.

Lucas was skirting a fine ethical line with Madame Zeldara, but his loophole was that he was not saving any of the data. It was used for carnival tricks only, nothing else.

But what else could it be used for?

"Daddy, I'm home!" she called as they reached the bottom of the basement stairs.

"Dana, my delectable offspring! And Ben," her father said, sitting up from his microscope. He ignored Bulk entirely, although he filled the stairwell behind Dana and Ben. Dr. Diamondback was in a white lab coat and suit, clothing he

still insisted on wearing even though he worked from home now. He squinted at Ben. "I have news for you, Ben!"

Dana pursed her lips and glanced at Ben, who stammered. She blew her bangs out of her eyes in disgust and spoke again, trying to capture her father's eyes. "What is it, Daddy?"

"I have been chosen!" He pulled a letter out of his coat pocket and waved it around. "The Emerald City Science Fair is in need of one more judge, and they have employed great intelligence in courting me to this post!"

"That's wonderful, Daddy!" Dana said, smiling widely. It was rare she saw her father so happy. She longed to someday make him react like that.

"But, uh, sir, won't S.K.Y. Labs people be there judging too?" asked Ben.

The glee left Diamondback's face as his grin vanished and his eyebrows furrowed. "That is correct, Ben. And?"

"Uh, well, you were, I mean, they . . . " Ben rubbed the back of his head and looked at Dana.

She gave him a disgusted look but decided to bail him out.

Dana took her father's arm again and pulled him backward, focusing on his computer monitor. "Daddy," she said loudly. "Is that a new nanovor? Did you discover it?"

"Clever one, my princess," he said, and Dana felt warm as she smiled back at him.

As the nanovor had distracted her father from his earlier annoyance about S.K.Y. Labs, Dana decided to take a chance. "Daddy, about the science fair. You know Lucas Nelson, the freshman who discovered the nanovor?"

He pursed his lips. "He remains fresh in my brain. Disappointing that negotiations with him have been unsuccessful."

Dana plastered on her special "Daddy" smile that she saved for only him. "Well, I think you and the S.K.Y. Labs judges should pay special attention to his science experiment."

Dr. Diamondback's eyes grew wide. "He's not exhibiting the nanovor, is he? I'll have his head if he reveals them to the scientific community before I do!"

Dana turned up the wattage on her smile. "No, Daddy. Nothing like that. But I really think it's something you need to see for yourself."

"Lucas is quite bright, I will grant him that. And if he could abandon his friendship with that appalling Sapphire, I might be willing to consider him a worthy disciple." He glanced at Ben and sneered a moment. Ben tried to stand up straighter. Dr. Diamondback shook his head. "But Lucas's refusal to aid me in the past gives me pause to grant him any special favor."

"What would you say if I said his science project may be the key to S.K.Y. Labs? Or rather, it's the door, and Lucas is the key. Would you give him more attention then?" Dana asked. Her cheeks felt flushed; she finally had her dad's full attention.

His eyes narrowed. "Tell me more."

Dana waited patiently by the door beside the two teachers guarding it.

"The science fair doesn't open until nine o'clock," the girls' gym teacher, Coach Albertson, said.

Dana sighed and blew her bangs back. She pulled her phone from her purse and sent a text to Nathan.

He appeared at the door in thirty seconds, poking his head out. "Sorry, Coach Albertson. We failed to get Dana her badge in time," he said, turning on his "charm the adult" smile.

The teacher relaxed considerably and said, "Of course, Nathan, but you know we have to abide by the rules. In you go, Ms. Diamondback."

Dana accepted the orange tag and lanyard from Nathan, only to have it snatched from her when she got inside the gym. "Thanks!" Dana said.

Nathan cast another look at her. "Sure, whatever, just don't cause any trouble."

"Wouldn't dream of it," she said, smiling.

The gymnasium had been transformed to seem almost county fair-like, with the different stalls each showing science projects. Dana passed a solar-system model and agricultural experiments better off in an elementary school fair. She also saw food booths with solar-powered popcorn poppers, homegrown rock candy, and a complicated Rube Goldberg-like machine.

She'd had a charming intro on the tip of her tongue, but she stopped short when she saw Lucas's booth.

A store mannequin torso, arms, and head rose from a white box. She wore a gypsy kerchief and had lightbulbs for eyes. Attached to the white box was a plaque:

MADAME ZELDARA

FORTUNE-TELLER

"Wow," she said.

Drew and Nathan stood with their backs to her, cleaning up the booth.

"So where's Mr. Sapphire? I figured he'd be here to cheer

Lucas on," Nathan asked Drew. He was polishing the plaque that bore Madame Zeldara's name. "Or at least help us set up."

Drew shrugged. "Lucas said he had an accident at home."

"Oh man, is it serious?"

"Not that kind of accident. One of his inventions went all insane on him. Spewed toothpaste all over the bathroom. I blame gremlins. He'll pull in sometime later, I expect."

Nathan laughed. "I thought he was supposed to be one of the greatest minds of his generation?"

Drew raised an eyebrow. "And have you never forgotten a line onstage, Romeo?"

Nathan shut his mouth with a click. After a moment he grinned and said, "Point taken."

Dana approached, purposely letting her feet fall heavily so they'd hear her. Nathan looked guarded. Drew squinted at her. "What is she doing here?" she asked Nathan.

Nathan shrugged. Dana smirked. "I caught a ride in with my dad. Hey, is Lucas around?"

Nathan jabbed his thumb down the line of stalls. "He's helping Mark Apple with his Twinkie experiment. Apparently, there was a disaster involving a hungry Boston terrier."

"That Lucas is a good guy," Dana said.

Drew glared at her. "You really think you need to tell us that?"

"Madame Zeldara is something else, isn't she?" asked Dana, circling the machine, casting her eyes over it.

"Dana, do you really need to be here? This is a private project," Drew said, her voice even.

"No, it isn't, not once the judges see it. They'll be so amazed this will be all over the Internet and papers. He's going to win for sure." Dana jiggled a locked door on the back of the white box.

"Hey," Drew said, grabbing Dana's arm. "Stay out of there."

"Calm down, freshman," Dana said coolly. "I just wanted to see how he put it together."

Nathan fidgeted with his badge. "Then maybe you should come back later when Lucas is here actually showing what Madame Zeldara can do."

Dana straightened and smiled at them both. "Oh I already know what she can do." They stared at her. "Yeah, Lucas showed me."

Their stunned silence was music to her ears. Nathan looked horrified, like he'd opened up the biggest box of worms, while Drew looked like she was preparing to sit Lucas down and wrap his ears around his head.

The tension was broken by Lucas, who came up behind Dana. "Hey Dana, I didn't know you'd be here early!"

Dana gave him a hug and pointed at Madame Zeldara. "That is amazing, Lucas. You're so going to beat the pants off of anyone else."

Lucas looked down, his ears turning red. "Hey, Drew, can you give me a hand down at Mark's booth? We need someone with a good mind for chemistry."

"Sure," Drew said. "It'll be good to stretch my legs anyway." She pointedly did not look at Dana as they left the booth.

Dana dropped her brilliant smile and faced Nathan. "Excellent. I didn't think we'd get this chance. Unlock that back door—I need to get to a data port."

"Wait, what?" Nathan raised his hands. "No way am I helping you sabotage Lucas's project."

She placed her hands on her hips. "Look, Nathan. I'm not going to sabotage anything. I told you, I want him to win. I just need to plug something into a data port. Or should I tell your precious freshman how the Snake Pit found out about the nanovor in the first place? Would you like them to know that?"

Nathan shrank under the blackmail, his broad shoulders slumping forward. "Fine. The key is in the front pocket of Lucas's backpack."

Her deft fingers opened the hinged door, and she grabbed a dongle out of her backpack, plugged it into a USB port, and plugged her phone into the other end.

"What are you doing, Dana?" Nathan sounded tired.

"Just a little data recording. The transmitter I just plugged in will send Zeldara's data to my phone. Nothing worse than pirating a song off the 'Net."

It was only a matter of time now. She had to find her dad.

Lucas fidgeted with the PARTICIPANT badge hanging from his orange lanyard. He moved to check Madame Zeldara again, but Drew stopped him.

"You mess with her any more, you are going to make her mad, Lucas," Drew said, her eyes dancing. "She wants to perform for you. You've tested her, she works, so just let her do her thing. And you do yours. You want to do this carnival style, do it right."

Lucas relaxed a little, his mind finally working through the empty panic, and saw his platform. At that moment, the doors opened and the crowds came in.

Lucas took a deep breath, and when he saw some classmates coming he belted out his best carnie impersonation. "Come one, come all! See the amazing fortune-teller

Madame Zeldara!"

"Oops—judges coming. Look lively," Nathan said.

Lucas scrambled to his feet and stepped out to meet Dr. Diamondback, sporting his yellow JUDGE badge proudly. Dana and Ben Arneson stood behind him silently, but Dana gave Lucas an encouraging smile.

He swallowed and said, "Dr. Diamondback, it's good to see you again."

"While I would like to say the same about the sight of you, alas I cannot," Dr. Diamondback said. He jotted a note of the participant number on Lucas's badge, sniffed once, then entered Lucas's booth. Not looking where he was going, he stood right on the red circle, scrutinizing Madame Zeldara.

"You have a robotic mannequin to show me? That's not terribly original, Lucas." He paused to write something on his electronic clipboard and moved to go to the next booth.

"BEWARE! BEWARE! BEWARE!" Madame Zeldara screeched. Lucas looked around in surprise; she had never reacted that way before. "Dr. Richard Diamondback! Beware!"

Diamondback's eyes narrowed, and he looked again at the machine. "Beware what?"

"Dr. Richard Diamondback, judge of Emerald City Science Fair, you do not think much of entries 498 or 481. You are formerly of S.K.Y. Lab Technologies, in charge of Research and Development, charged with falsifying test results, encouraged to step down from that position. Repeated attempts to communicate with S.K.Y. Lab Technologies have proven unsuccessful. Currently, Madame Zeldara predicts the next email you send will have a 91 percent chance of also failing to achieve the communication you desire. Madame Zeldara's advice: Do not attempt to contact S.K.Y. Lab Technologies again."

Lucas winced. Madame Zeldara clearly had a definite chance to anger her subjects, which was not exactly his goal.

"How did you get such information?" Dr. Diamondback said through gritted teeth.

"Madame Zeldara scans your face and runs facial-recognition software, then goes to the 'Net to see what information is available, then scans your mobile devices, like that clipboard or your phone, where it saw your email, and it gets more information on you. Then it runs probability matrices to figure out the likelihood of any number of things."

Dr. Diamondback's eyes went wide and focused beyond

Lucas for a moment. He fumbled on, saying, "None of the information is—"

Diamondback didn't wait to hear the rest. He stalked from the booth, fuming. Dana and Ben followed.

"That . . . didn't go as well as I had hoped," Lucas said, deflating.

Applause erupted from the aisle, and he looked up to see three judges, all wearing collared shirts with S.K.Y. Lab Technologies on the breast. They'd tucked their clipboards under their arms and were clapping for Lucas. One, a tall woman, stepped forward and extended her hand.

"That was amazing. Lucas, is it?" she asked. Lucas nodded, his eyes wide as he shook her hand. "I'm Dr. Susan Hatch. I'm in charge of the intern program at S.K.Y. Labs. With me are Dr. Waits, in charge of R&D, and Dr. McCloud, a physicist on his team. We heard most of what you told Dr. Diamondback but would like to ask some more questions."

Lucas shook the men's hands. "Do you want to see a demonstration?"

Dr. Waits raised his hand, "I'll do it."

Lucas held his breath as Madame Zeldara shouted for the elderly Dr. Waits to BEWARE about serving potato salad to guests again, as his email indicated that many friends got food poisoning soon after his latest cookout. His colleagues laughed at him and he exited the red circle, grinning.

"I guess I deserved that," he said.

Lucas grinned and looked down. "Yeah, I don't control what info Madame Zeldara grabs."

"This is fascinating technology, Lucas, but the privacy concerns are not small," said Dr. Waits, squinting at the data sheet on Madame Zeldara.

"Oh, no, none of the data is stored. It's just used for fun."

"That was a good move," Dr. Hatch said. "You're young for a device of this complexity, younger than we usually go for interns. But, depending on the outcome of the science fair, if we were to contact you for an internship, would you be open to the idea?"

Lucas's jaw dropped. "Uh, yes, totally, of course."

A motion caught his eye, and he saw Drew, frantically waving at him and pointing at Madame Zeldara.

"Uh." He took a look at Madame Zeldara, who looked fine.

"Very impressive, Lucas. We may be in touch soon," Dr. Hatch said. The judges all shook his hand again and left the booth.

"Nice to meet you," he said, waving at them.

The moment they were gone, Drew ran over to him and grabbed his arm. "Lucas, we have some serious juju to deal with."

"What's wrong?" he asked, his ears still ringing with the word "internship."

"There's something you need to know. Something about Madame Zeldara."

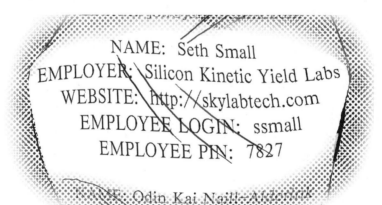

NAME: Seth Small
EMPLOYER: Silicon Kinetic Yield Labs
WEBSITE: http://skylabtech.com
EMPLOYEE LOGIN: ssmall
EMPLOYEE PIN: 7827

E: Odin Kai Naill-A

Drew's hand was like a vice on Lucas's wrist. "Hey, wait a minute!" he yelled as she dragged him along the aisle to behind the caramel-apple booth. The machine churned happily to itself, ticking and sproinging, nearly masking the noise around them. Drew pushed Lucas's head down so they were behind the back wall.

"What's—" Lucas started, but Drew put a hand over his mouth. Her hand smelled of lavender soap.

Drew pushed her face right next to his. "Hush. Snake Pit. Listen."

She removed her hand, and Lucas, in confusion, focused on the voices behind them.

Ben's voice came through the noise of the machine muffled, as if he were eating. "Mates. Musshaf been im email."

"Right . . . all . . . here."

"Joo get im . . . records?"

"God, Ben, can you . . . talk with . . . mouth full?" Dana's voice dripped with disdain.

"Shorry."

"If you're . . . about the personal . . . yeah, I can see Waits's . . ."

Lucas's eyes went wide. "What are they talking about?" he mouthed.

Drew put her finger over her own lips and continued to listen.

Ben's voice was finally clear. "What . . . discover, anyway?"

Dana was silent for a moment. "Looks like a. . . perpetual. . . machine. Has to be . . . in space. . . . will be expensive. Millions worth. But . . . worth billions."

"So what now?"

The machine made a horrible coughing sound and stopped working, and Ben yelped in pain. The owner of the project gave a despairing cry and came over to fix it, but Lucas and Drew could still hear Dana, finally clearly.

"Easy. We'll use the information I got from hacking Lucas's fortune-teller machine. I've gotten the passwords for S.K.Y. Labs' servers. I'll go into the nanosphere, use the nanovor to get past any security I don't have passwords for, and plant this information I cooked up last night in Dr. Waits's files. I can indicate that he worked with my dad a while back and stole this information from him. He'll get fired, Daddy has his job back. Simple."

Lucas's eyes went wide. He and Drew scrambled behind the next booth over.

"What in the world are they talking about? They're not..." Lucas trailed off, the horror dawning on him.

Drew's face was intense. "Somehow Dana got the information Madame Zeldara grabbed and used it to get further into S.K.Y. Labs' internal files, Lucas. Madame Zeldara's been hacked. Looks like Dana's going to steal Waits's latest discovery and use it to get her dad back into his position at S.K.Y. Labs."

"Oh no," he whispered. The whole crushing realization that this could be his fault—and what he would lose if caught—came down on him, and he felt slightly dizzy.

Drew dragged him out into the hallway and stuffed her backpack into her locker, then turned back to Lucas.

"Hey," she said, lightly patting his cheeks. "Come back to

me. We have to turn off Madame Zeldara. We don't know what else she's grabbing."

"Wait a second, just let me think," Lucas said. "We aren't one hundred percent sure that's what's going on, right? I mean, Dana could be getting that information elsewhere."

Lucas thought Drew would hit him. "Are you seriously that dense? You're honestly going to tell me that you built that machine but you can't add one and one?"

Lucas lowered his voice to a desperate whisper and turned to look back at Madame Zeldara. "Drew, if this is my fault, then I could get in serious trouble. It's not my intention or Madame Zeldara's design to do this. I could lose the fair and the internship. We need to check and make sure that it's not caused by something else. Will you give me that?"

He turned back toward her. "Drew?"

But she was gone.

Dana's glee was barely contained as she slipped her second touch-screen phone into her purse. This one connected to the one linked to Madame Zeldara and downloaded all captured data.

"That's a cool idea, Dana. But can your phone upload all that data? You can't break in like Madame Zeldara did," Ben asked, licking the caramel from his fingers.

"Not from here, no. But I can get into the S.K.Y. Labs secure servers from the nanosphere. The nanovor eat most firewalls and other types of computer security for lunch. And since all the geeks are in here going gaga over the science fair, I can get in there with no hassle.

Dana looked around. No one paid them any attention, so she led Ben casually toward the gymnasium exit.

"But you've got to do more than just upload the files, right?" Ben asked softly. "I mean S.K.Y. Labs could just find out and decide to keep the information private and give him a slap on the wrist. You're going to have to make sure this happens in public so he can be embarrassed and your dad gets reinstated, right?"

"It's simple, Ben, really," Dana said. She stopped beside the hydroponic-corn project. "Daddy makes sure Lucas wins so he can take Madame Zeldara to the state competition. The same judges will also be at state, and when Lucas does the experiment on Dr. Waits again, Madame Zeldara will tell everyone about the machine and Daddy."

"How do you know she'll choose that?"

Dana thought for a moment. "It seems Madame Zeldara chooses the most recent bits of info she can get. Daddy just wrote the email to S.K.Y. Labs this morning. Waits may have just gotten word about the bad potato salad. It's a risk we have to take. I can date the data to be next Saturday morning, same day of the state science fair, so that should stack the odds in our favor. I need to get to the nanosphere to upload this new data. I'll go find a quiet place to sit while I go into the nanosphere. It'll only take five minutes, tops."

Dana and Ben turned the corner around the final science project, the sadly ignored hydroponic corn, where she nearly ran into Drew.

The freshman was crouched down as if hiding, and her eyes were wide as Dana stumbled to a stop in front of her.

Drew stood and gave an impish grin. "Don't suppose you'd like to have your fortune told, would you?"

Dana's voice was very controlled, although she wanted to reach out and throttle the younger girl. "Ben. Make sure she doesn't bother me in the nanosphere."

Drew turned and bolted down the aisle, dodging students, parents, judges, and one Boston terrier, which was running full tilt for its own reasons, a Twinkie in its mouth.

Dana glared at Ben. "Well? Get her!"

Ben took off, calling for Bulk to join him.

Dana sighed and exited the gym to find an empty classroom.

Lucas wasn't able to turn Madame Zeldara off when he got back to the booth, as two impatient students were waiting there for him. His mind reeled as he put one of them in the red circle without any of his carnie preamble, ignoring their amazed faces as Madame Zeldara warned them that the movie they wanted to see this weekend was nearly sold out.

A shout and commotion came from across the hall, and Lucas moved into the aisle to see what the fuss was. He winced as he saw a streak of chestnut followed by a blond and black blur, and then the hydroponic-corn project fell over.

Cries of "Hey!" and "Ow!" and "Stop her!" came closer, and Lucas still couldn't tell what was going on. A group of kids gathered in front of him to look at Madame Zeldara, so when the tidal wave hit him he never saw it coming.

He was down on the floor before he saw who it was.

Drew was already scrambling to her feet and pulling him up as well. She reached out and grabbed his nametag, whirled her head around, and said, "Come on. We have to find Nathan," before she began pulling him behind her.

"But the booth, Madame Zeldara. Drew, what's going on?" Lucas said, but she didn't answer.

They dodged some girls who texted furiously on their cell phones, and Drew turned a corner, then looked back frantically. The girls screamed then, and Lucas saw one of the cell phones fly into the air.

"Well, not as much of a lead as I'd thought," she muttered and was off again.

Track was Drew's specialty, definitely not Lucas's, and he slowed her down considerably, but she refused to let go.

"You wanna tell me why we're running so fast?" asked Lucas.

"First tell me where Nathan is!" she said, stopping and looking around frantically.

"Oh, I think he said something about those caramel apples," Lucas gasped, remembering. He looked behind them.

Ben Arneson and Bulk Damage dashed for them.

"Oh, man, I get it. Let's go!" Lucas yelled, and they were off again.

Lucas hoped that the judges had already been by the exhibits that Ben and Bulk destroyed in their wake. Drew led him into the booth with the replica of the solar system, delicately dodging marbles and Ping-Pong balls painted to look like planets, then jumped on the table in the back of the booth and vaulted over the side. Lucas followed with more apologizing and less grace.

The caramel-apple display was in front of them then, and Nathan stood there stupidly agape, apple in hand.

"Nathan!" Drew yelled. She reached him and flung Lucas's slightly buttery nametag over his head. "You have to go back to the booth and be Lucas for a while. We have something we need to do."

"But, I don't know—" Nathan said.

Drew set her jaw as Ben and Bulk's yells came closer. "Look. Are you an actor?"

"Well, yeah," said Nathan.

"Do you know how to work Madame Zeldara?"

"Sure."

"Then go be Lucas!"

He finally nodded. Ben and Bulk rounded a corner. Lucas winced when he heard, "There she is!"

"And here we go!" Drew said. She took off again, Lucas behind her. "I have an idea, Lucas. Follow me."

"Like I have a choice?" he said. They took a sharp right turn, then another. Lucas realized they were running in circles. They passed his booth, luckily leaving it unscathed. Nathan stood there proudly showing off Madame Zeldara when something popped in Lucas's mind. In his nearly total panic, he'd found a bright spot in realizing what could be causing Madame Zeldara's problems. He grabbed for his cell phone in his front pocket and hit the N speed-dial button for Nathan.

"Yeah?" Nathan said. "It's Lucas," he began.

"Dude, what did you two do? You've busted up the whole science fair!"

"Nathan, the only way Madame Zeldara could be saving data and transmitting it is if there's something plugged into one of her data ports. You have to check her data ports, in the back, and remove anything you see. Do you understand?"

Nathan said something that sounded like, "Oh, yeah, got

it. It's out," but Lucas couldn't be sure as he had to shut his phone and hold his arm up to stop a tall wooden structure—half a catapult—from falling on him.

"They're getting closer, Drew. Are we going to run around in circles this whole time?" he said. "They'll catch us eventually."

As if on cue, a large crash sounded behind them, and Lucas risked a peek. Bulk lay on the carpet, sprawled over the downed catapult. Ben ran on, leaving his friend.

"Or maybe not," Lucas said.

They neared the caramel-apple machine again. "Lucas!" Drew shouted. "Keep running toward the exit to the cafeteria!"

"Got it!" Lucas yelled. Drew pulled up at the caramel-apple machine, and Lucas shot ahead past her. He heard a crash and a despairing yell and a hasty, "I'm sorry!"

Then there was a surprised howl that sounded like Ben and a loud thump.

Drew caught up with him easily, and, with his hand on the door, Lucas chanced a look back.

Ben sat on the carpet, covered in caramel, with a weeping student behind him looking at the ruins of her Rube Goldberg device. Lucas hoped she'd get second place, because it really was a cool machine.

Drew pulled him through the door. "He won't be long. There. Janitor's closet. Let's go."

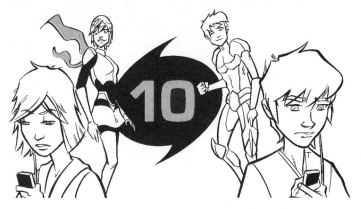

Lucas and Drew shut the door behind them and tried to slow their panicked breathing in silence.

They didn't need to worry. When Ben and Bulk Damage plowed through, they made enough noise coming through the door and looking up and down the hallway and complained so loudly that Lucas and Drew could have had a full-volume conversation in the closet and Ben and Bulk wouldn't have heard them.

Not that they took that chance. They stood frozen, breathing as carefully as they could and trying not to upset the mops and buckets that they found themselves straddling.

"They should be trailing as much stuff as we are. See if you can see anything," they heard Ben say in an outraged voice.

"I don't think they're trailing as much caramel as you,"

Bulk said.

"Sure, laugh it up. That's helping," said Ben. "They probably went to go hide in Mr. Sapphire's classroom. Whatever we do, we have to keep them away from Dana."

"Why?"

"Why do you think, you idiot? She's hitting the nanosphere to upload that data she got."

"Oh. Why don't we just guard Dana?"

Ben's voice had the impatient-patient tone that many parents used when dealing with slow children. "Because—"

"Wait up, man. I busted up my ankle on that wooden thing," Bulk said.

Lucas snickered at the whining tone in his voice, but Drew punched his shoulder.

Ben and Bulk's footsteps faded into the distance and up the stairs. Risking another punch from Drew, Lucas let out a huge breath.

"So you wanna tell me what was going on back there?" he asked her.

She shifted uncomfortably in the closet, edging closer to him. "You mean besides getting half the school mad at me? Yeah. I overheard Dana making plans to upload this false

data using the nanosphere. I know you don't believe they used Madame Zeldara—"

"No," Lucas interrupted quietly. "You're right. It was my invention. It let them download and store the private information. Now they're going to do something bad with it. I have to stop them."

Drew put her hand on his shoulder, and he froze. "You have to stop her, Lucas. Dana's the only one in the nanosphere. I'm not trying to harp on you or say I told you so, but I want you to know what we're facing. Dana is in there, Dana stole the data, and Dana is the one uploading the false data to get her dad's job back. Do you understand?"

He was silent for a moment. She removed her hand from his shoulder. "I'm glad you're going to do what's right, and I'm sorry if it ruins your chances to go to the state science fair next weekend. But Dana is also planning on rigging the contest so you win and go to state, and she's going to use Madame Zeldara to expose Dr. Waits. She thinks she has to make a big public stink about it to make her daddy smell like roses."

Lucas sighed. "Would it really be so bad if I at least got the credit for inventing the machine that exposed the bad guy from S.K.Y. Labs?"

Drew poked him in the back of the head. "Yes, it would be so bad! He's not really a bad guy! He's being framed! This would be like you getting kicked out of school because someone pretended to prove you didn't create Madame Zeldara. Would that be fair?"

Lucas shook his head in the dark, knowing she wouldn't see him.

"And besides," she continued, "heroes don't do it for credit. They do things because they're right. Sometimes no one even knows who saved the day. The point is that the right thing gets done."

"Yeah, yeah," he said, sighing. "You and your 'doing the right thing' thing." She had a point, no matter how much he didn't like to admit it. He could always count on Drew to see the right thing to do, and he ended up better because of it.

He surprised them both by turning and hugging her in the dark closet. "Thanks for being there," he said.

"Oh, hey, sure, no problem," she said, taken aback.

"Drew?" he said, still hugging her.

"Yeah?" She barely breathed.

"You have popcorn in your hair."

She shoved him off her, laughing. "Come on. Let's go after Dana."

They fumbled in the dark to get their nanoscopes from their book bags. Doc Zap had modified them to connect to the nanosphere via wifi, so they didn't have to be near the nanoscanner to enter the 'sphere. They each slipped on their earphones and turned them on.

The "earphones" were actually headsets that tapped into their wearers' brainwaves. With their headsets in place, Lucas and Drew would be able to project into the nanosphere and control avatars there that could interact with the nanoscopic landscape the nanovor called home.

As their headsets pulled them into the nanosphere, Drew whispered to Lucas, "I got your back, Lucas."

"I know, Drew."

Dana arrived in the nanosphere with two of her nanovor waiting for her already. She walked toward them across spiky, iridescent blue grass that crunched with a flat, digital sound as she crushed the blades. The sleek blue Megadoom munched contentedly on the grass while her deadly aqua-colored Doom Mantis—a nanovor that looked like it walked on knives instead of legs—watched her approach. Her favorite, the serpentlike Phase Spiker, wasn't here yet.

"Are you ladies ready to make some history?" she asked. Although the nanovor never exhibited any signs that they were one gender or another, she'd gotten tired of the boys calling all of their nanovor "him," so she had decided hers were female. She also called all of Ben's nanovor "her," just to annoy him.

She patted the sleek armor of the Megadoom. For being a violent silicon-based creature, it showed a good deal of affection for Dana. It nuzzled her, and she pushed it off gently. She concentrated briefly, and energy crackled in her hands—the electric leash they used to control the nanovor within the nanosphere. She held one hand out to each nanovor, and the leashes leaped from her hands to capture the creatures.

Her avatar wore a black bodysuit, showing curves that seemed more serpentine than feminine. From a deep pocket within her red cloak she pulled a wriggling snake. It was blue and twined around her wrist like a bracelet. She whispered a Web address to it and dropped it into the sharp grass. It slithered off, and Dana followed it at a jog.

Data appeared in unfamiliar forms in the nanosphere. The snake was actually a program that would locate the S.K.Y. Labs servers for her.

Databases loomed in the distance like crystalline structures, but the snake avoided those and stuck to the fields between the fortresses. Dana leaped over a crimson data stream, a chat room for fans of the latest teen star. Usually she would stick around and listen in, but she had no time.

Dana loved the nanosphere. The power she had over other

avatars and nanovor was unique; she'd modified the nanoscanner to increase her power when she created her avatar. Unfortunately, this modification made her power in the 'sphere as unreliable as it was strong. But she didn't have to be here for long; she had only one job to do, and that didn't include fighting any nanovor or messing with others' avatars.

The snake slowed, nearing a mountain range. While most databases were fortresses, the stronger governmental or large-corporation databases were made of actual mountains of data. Rocky outcroppings of Web pages sat on top while huge humming collections of data lay within.

Dana approached the first blocked mountain pass, an iron gate that stretched twenty feet high and off in either direction. She knew from experience that if she tried to scale the fence, or tried to get a nanovor to fly her over, the gate would only stretch higher. It was only a representation of data; there was no way to get past it without the password.

Thank goodness for Madame Zeldara. Dana slipped her hand into her pocket again and pulled out a golden skeleton key: password number one. It slid easily into the lock in the gate. When she turned it, the entire gate and fence disappeared, flickering briefly before it went.

"Welcome to S.K.Y. Lab Technologies," a pleasant voice said.

"Thank you very much," Dana said and continued further. Two passwords to go, according to the information she had from Madame Zeldara.

She was walking on a steep mountain road now. If she stopped and concentrated on the rock surrounding her, she could make out the internal Web pages of S.K.Y. Labs. But she wasn't where she needed to be, so she led her nanovor on.

The second gate blocked the actual entrance to the mountain, a round grate set into the rock. It didn't seem to need a key, but there was a button to press. She didn't know how to get to the button without impaling her arm, since if you were injured in the nanosphere, it affected your body in the real world. She wasn't sure of the extent of the injury she'd carry—Lucas had been hit by a nanovor attack in the arm once and it had been numb for days after—but she wasn't going to test it if she didn't need to.

She reached into her pocket for the second password. It appeared as a chainmail glove that stretched up her arm. She pulled the heavy glove on and reached in. A spike snagged on her glove, but as it got lodged in the chainmail, it flickered and died. Once she'd removed most of the spikes, she was free to reach the button and push it.

Like the other gate, it disappeared completely.

The gate protected a narrow tunnel, lit by torches that burned a deep green—data gathered from experiments, numbers that meant something only when connected to a project. It would be good to farm that data, but she didn't have the time.

At the end of the tunnel, Dana stepped out into another field full of blue grass. A yellow river ran through the center, streams of data going out into the Internet. And beyond the river, a crystalline wall surrounded a fortress. The thick seal looked impenetrable, but she wasn't worried; Madame Zeldara would come through.

She slid her hand into her pocket again and closed her fingers around nothing. Snakes that served as her data carriers or her address locators slithered around her fingers, but she couldn't find a password.

Why wasn't the third password in there? Madame Zeldara should have had it! She stood back from the wall and thought.

Lucas must have found the phone plugged into the fortune-teller and removed it. Ben and Bulk had failed her.

Her Megadoom nuzzled her again, and she patted it absently.

"Well, girl, looks like it's down to a 'vor. We can probably use you, but best to start with the big guns, huh?"

It made a low, digital sound. Dana concentrated and sent an electric charge through the nanosphere, the call leaving her hands like lightning. Her favorite nanovor was not one that treated her with doglike affection like the other two. This one refused to be tamed, working with her only out of mutual respect. But when she needed a lot of power, it was where she turned first.

Phase Spiker, her blue and green viperlike 'vor, appeared close to her. It rumbled at her, and she patted it gently. She pointed at the crystal wall and said, "Do you think you can take that down?"

She didn't need to encourage it further. It rushed at the wall, lunging with an Asp Kiss attack. She stepped back as the crystal wall gave a deafening ringing noise, like chimes. Dana covered her ears as it lunged again. The crystal remained strong and unyielding.

She chewed on her lip for a moment, then, with a motion

of her hand, sent in the other nanovor. Her armored Mega-doom charged forward, and the spindly Doom Mantis began jabbing its swordlike legs at the crystal.

The noise was terrific, and Dana backed up to watch. The Doom Mantis achieved the first breaking point, its sharp feet causing a crack in the crystal.

"Almost there! Come on!" she yelled. Her Phase Spiker lashed out again and the crystal wall flickered.

"Yes." Dana took one step forward, grinning in anticipation. But then she heard something behind her.

"Dana! Stop!"

Dana turned slowly to face Lucas and Drew. As much as he didn't want to, Lucas marveled at her avatar.

The red cloak streamed from her shoulders, and her sinewy body looked coiled and ready to strike. Her black bodysuit turned to an angry red, her cloak turning deep reddish brown, the color of old blood.

He gulped. Dana's avatar always shifted with her mood in the nanosphere, and this didn't bode well. Her normally green eyes now glowed with a reddish light. Her alien beauty seemed more nanovor than human. Lucas and Drew retained their human figures with their avatars, only adding armor, while Dana's lengthening fangs made her look like a snake goddess.

He looked over the landscape. They appeared to be in the

middle of an arena, an area in the nanosphere where formal nanovor battles took place. That was good. If their nanovor died here, they would regenerate. Elsewhere in the nanosphere, they would risk losing them permanently.

Drew was not distracted by Dana's beauty or power over the nanosphere. She was a girl of action as her hands crackled with energy. Her own nanovor, having heard the summons, appeared beside her.

"Time to make the doughnuts," Drew said and sent her nanovor at Dana's. Plasma Lash, the six-legged nanovor sporting a large tentacle on its head; Tank Strider, the yellow armored 'vor that always reminded Lucas of a school bus of doom; and Plasma Locust, the thin, quick, six-legged blue 'vor, all rushed forward to engage Dana's nanovor, which were still attacking the firewall.

Dana pulled the Megadoom and Doom Mantis off the firewall and put them in front of her to meet the assault.

Drew punched Lucas in the arm. "Hello? Did you make it in or are you stuck halfway? Remember the plan? Scary snake girl! Must stop her!"

Lucas rubbed his arm. "Right. I was distracted. That's some impressive . . . security."

Drew made a disgusted noise. Lucas busied himself summoning his own nanovor. They appeared after a minute: his trusty Storm Spinner, the floating Storm Hunter, and another graceful Plasma Lash. He sent them at Dana's swarm.

Dana didn't look scared at the six nanovor coming against her two. Behind her, the Phase Spiker still attacked the crystal wall, and the loud chimes were starting to sound distorted as the security weakened.

"Lucas, what's the point?" she called. "You know you're too late! I'm going to get through and upload this information. And if you expose what I did, you will get in trouble for Madame Zeldara's data stealing. If you help me instead, I guarantee you'll win this science fair, and I can probably rig you winning state, too."

"Listen to yourself!" yelled Drew. "Lucas doesn't want to win a rigged game!"

Lucas let them argue, concentrating on sending his Storm Hunter at Dana's Megadoom, the two exchanging blows. Drew sent her own Tank Strider scuttling toward Dana's Doom Mantis for a straight-on head butt.

The crystal wall shuddered behind them and flickered once. Lucas pulled his Storm Hunter back a bit, his energy

leash growing tight. He was trying to lure the Megadoom away from Dana. It followed and threw itself on the Storm Hunter, lashing out and cutting great hunks from his nanovor. The Storm Hunter sputtered wetly and melted back into the nanosphere.

"Drew, we have to end this now. Go after the Phase Spiker. I'll take care of the other two."

"But you're down one!"

"That's not important. The Phase Spiker is important."

Drew nodded then and sent her 'vor rushing past Dana to distract and take down the Phase Spiker.

Dana's nanovor still attacked the wall with single-minded intensity, resorting to body slamming it. The wall shook with each blast. Dana's Plasma Locust hit the Phase Spiker with a Plasma Blast, weakening it, as the Plasma Lash struck with a Head Whip.

Dana's avatar glowed even brighter red, and even though Lucas knew they had the upper hand, he took two steps back as she seemed to grow before him. It was an illusion, he figured, as she snapped back to her normal size and ran for the yellow river a couple of steps away, dodging away from the crystal wall. She slipped a hand inside her cloak and brought out a tiny black snake. She whispered something to it and dropped it into the data stream, where it stood out starkly from the yellow data.

"So what was that?" asked Lucas. "You can't have uploaded the info from here."

Dana smirked. "You'll find out soon enough. You're not the only one who can turn a fight unfair."

"Unfair? What do you mean? You're the one who hacked my science project!"

A squeal and a squelch sounded from the battle, and they both turned to see Lucas's Plasma Lash finish whipping through the Doom Mantis's body with its tentacle. Lucas relaxed a little. Her nanovor were falling. They'd have this won in a moment.

Dana hissed and yanked on the leash attached to her Phase Spiker. It turned from attacking Drew's wounded Plasma Lash and launched itself at the wall. Unfortunately, it was that moment when Drew's Tank Strider came in for a head butt and pushed the Phase Spiker further into the wall, crushing the nanovor but putting its own momentum into the wall. The crystal wall flickered again and vanished.

"There you two are. We've been looking for you," said a

voice behind Lucas.

He winced and turned around. Ben and Bulk Damage stood there, their avatars smiling, their nanovor already summoned and waiting behind them like soldiers.

Bulk Damage slammed his fist into his palm. "Time for the second half."

ot your text, Dana," Ben said. "You didn't say you were getting double-teamed by some freshmen."

Lucas looked impressed despite himself. "Dana, that snake was a text message? You can send text messages from inside the nanosphere? How—"

Dana ignored him and snarled at Ben. "You weren't smart enough to catch them outside, but I thought you might be able to take care of them in the nanosphere if I handed them to you. Just keep them busy. I need to get this data uploaded!"

Dana was pleased to see Lucas lose his bravado when faced with Ben and Bulk. He gulped and tugged on his remaining two nanovor to exit the battle with Dana's Megadoom. They reluctantly returned to his side. Dana considered sending her Megadoom after them, but she figured Ben and Bulk's six nanovor against Lucas's two stacked the odds enough in her favor.

But there was also Drew. Dana felt her last leash go slack as her Megadoom exploded in a messy torrent, the victim of an Arc Blast from Dana's sneaky Plasma Locust. She edged away.

Ben sent his Spike Spine toward Lucas, but it was blown backward by another Arc Blast from Drew's Plasma Locust, which had dashed forward to put itself between Lucas and the approaching nanovor. Spent, it rushed back and let Drew's Plasma Lash take its place beside Lucas's nanovor.

"Drew, watch Bulk's Doom Blade. Keep it away from the others!" said Lucas, throwing his Plasma Lash in front of Ben's Gamma Fury. The two began to trade blows, and Lucas pushed his Storm Spinner in front of Bulk's Battle Kraken, preparing for the next round.

Drew positioned her nanovor to aid Lucas's, sending her Plasma Locust around to attack Ben and Bulk's nanovor with Plasma Blasts, draining some of their strength.

Unfortunately she caught Lucas's Plasma Lash in the blast.

"Drew!" Lucas yelled in annoyance.

"Collateral damage! Friendly fire happens. My bad!" she

said, reining in the Plasma Locust and instead pushing her Plasma Lash to attack Bulk's Doom Blade with its wickedly swift tentacle. Next, her Tank Strider lumbered through the melee, slamming into enemy nanovor, knocking some down.

Bulk's Electrobull charged her Tank Strider, and the two hulking creatures stood there like garbage trucks facing off. Suddenly, they rushed each other, connecting with a loud *BLAM!* that generated a pressure wave that knocked everyone down.

Dana edged closer to the door the crystal wall had been guarding. Drew whipped her head around and spotted Dana, who finally took off at a run.

"Lucas, go after her! I can handle these guys!" Drew yelled.

Dana didn't wait to hear his response. She was through the door and down the hall before she knew what had happened in the battle.

The hallway led to one room with multiple pools of water set into the floor like hot tubs. Dana peered at the data briefly and determined which one would hold Dr. Waits's files. Pulling snakes from her pockets, she dumped them into the data pools. Green, blue, black, and yellow snakes all slithered and wriggled and swam in circles, starting their uploads: text files and images and altered photographs that Dana had been saving for weeks, waiting to get an opportunity like this.

Her father had told her about the early days of the Internet with dial-up modems, and she hadn't believed anything could be that slow. She believed it now, waiting for the little snakes to slip deep into the pools. A couple dipped below the surface but still continued to swim around in a circle.

"Oh, no freaking way are you getting away with that!" Lucas yelled from the hallway. His Storm Spinner was with him, and he sent it charging toward her. Although it was unlike nanovor to attack humans directly, one didn't stare down a huge bug with a razor-sharp blade on its face. Dana yelled and scrambled back out of its way.

The Storm Spinner ran by her. It leaped into the data pool and darted around, its mandibles snaring the data snakes from the water and chopping them to pieces.

"No!" screamed Dana. But with no nanovor at her call, she could only watch as Lucas's Storm Spinner splashed and sliced, kicking up the data pool until it was frothy. It submerged itself briefly and came back up, a black snake caught it in its jaw. It was the largest and had the most important piece of information—the fact that Waits had stolen the perpetual-motion machine schematics from her father.

She watched mutely as the snake disappeared down the nanovor's gullet and tried not to cry. All her plans, ruined.

The Storm Spinner lunged out of the pool and wandered over to where Lucas was studying the wall of the room, which looked like it was made of a crystal honeycomb. Dana got on her hands and knees and peered into the data pool, wondering if there was a way she could replicate the data.

She glanced over at Lucas. He had his hand, fingers splayed, on one of the hexagons. He turned it briefly, and it clicked three times. "There," he said.

The black snake had started to form again in her hands as she arranged the data into another uploadable file, but Lucas grabbed her arm. "No time for that. The firewall is coming back, and you don't want to be stuck in here when it does."

The wall clicked twice more. The crystals along the wall turned from clear to yellow.

"Lucas, you can't stop me. I have to do this!" Dana cried.

The wall clicked once. The crystals glowed red. Lucas

ordered his nanovor out of the room, pushed Dana out the door, and dove after her.

"Run!"

She finally understood. She didn't want to be caught in there when the crystal wall was reinstated. The crystal wall flickered ahead of them, causing the cave to go dark for an instant.

"Oh no," said Lucas, picking up the pace.

With a screech, the Storm Spinner leaped from the tunnel and skidded to a stop at the entrance. "It's blocking our way!" yelled Dana.

The Storm Spinner rose up to its full height. The wall flickered again. "No! Under it!" yelled Lucas, and he and Dana dove from the tunnel under the Storm Spinner as the wall became solid again. A nanosecond later the Storm Spinner split in two, the wall neatly cutting it in half. It fell off the wall and melted back into the nanosphere.

Dana and Lucas lay on the grass, panting. Dana watched the half-formed black data snake disintegrate in front of her eyes.

She heard a triumphant whoop and opened her eyes. Drew was pumping her fist in the air, grinning, her three nanovor by her side. Dana could barely make out Ben and

Bulk beyond her, looking stunned.

"Yeah!" Drew yelled. "You RUN from the Battle Mastah! That's BAT-TLE MAS-TAH. Learn it, live it, love it! That's right, boys, you battled a girl and LOST!"

Dana closed her eyes again. Could it get any worse than this?

Lucas came over to her and stood over her. "Are you okay?"

Her eyes flew open, and she was on her feet in an instant, looking him in the eye. She clenched her fists. "Am I okay? I get a perfect chance to restore Daddy's job, and you ruin it! And what I don't get is that I was even helping you win the science fair at the same time. Now you might even get into trouble for saving that data! No, I'm pretty freaking far from okay!"

She could feel her control on her avatar slipping, as her words sounded more like hisses and her avatar glowed red.

Lucas looked at her, then the ground.

"Listen, Lucas. You just lost one of the biggest chances you ever had with me. My friendship, my connection with my father and S.K.Y. Labs, are—"

She'd never get a chance to tell Lucas what they were, because a loud hiss sounded from the other side of the river, cutting her off.

Dana had heard that hiss before. She wanted to break down the crystal wall and hide inside. She knew what that hiss meant. Then it spoke its own name.

"Sssssspyyydraaannn."

Dana's avatar turned molten in front of Lucas as she screamed. He found himself feeling a bit of pity for her. He knew she had betrayed him, but Dana was always so cool, so collected; this kind of temper tantrum had to be because of how utterly defeated she was.

When she stopped, her eyes got wide, and her avatar went from red to gray as if someone had turned a switch, Lucas's heart rate quickened. Dana wasn't afraid of much. Really, the only thing he knew that she was honestly afraid of was—

"Sssssspyyydraaannn."

Lucas looked over to where Drew had stopped gloating at Ben and Bulk. All three stared at whatever was behind him. "So much for hoping for a bluff," he muttered and turned around.

He'd seen Spydran before, but it always shocked him

when he did. Nanovor—especially when viewed "actual size" in the nanosphere—could look pretty freaky, but compared to Spydran, the other nanovor looked like fluffy kitties. In relation to the humans' size in the nanosphere, Spydran stood about twelve feet high. Heavy armor covered its six limbs, and its body vaguely resembled that of a hyena, with two powerful legs extending from its shoulders in front, and two shorter, weaker legs (with equally wicked claws) coming from its hips. Two clawed arms rose up and out of its torso, giving its already impressive height the illusion of added stature.

Spydran tapped experimentally on the crystal wall with a claw. The wall rang loudly through the open field like a bell, and the humans put hands to their ears. "Interrogative: Where is the other wall?"

It spied Lucas and took a step forward. Lucas could swear the ground shook, even though the ground was made of pure data.

"You," Spydran said, with a truckload of malice directed in one word at Lucas. "Lucas flesh-thing. You are interfering again. Why?"

"I—" Lucas was hesitant to say he had been following

Dana, trying to stop her from interfering in the nanosphere. Whatever she had done, she didn't deserve to be handed to Spydran on a plate.

Spydran took another step forward. "Great power would have been needed to remove the security wall. Why are you interfering?"

While Lucas talked to Spydran, Dana ran silently to Ben and Bulk. She grabbed her friends' arms and yelled, "You two have fun. We're out of here."

Spydran took two quick steps in their direction but hissed as they disappeared out of the nanosphere.

Lucas sighed, his stomach sour. He had been stupid to think that they would all fight Spydran together, even though he'd been prepared to defend them.

The massive nanovor sensei reared to its full height. "Observation: You do not control your human swarm well."

Lucas laughed, a short, barking sound that sounded false to him. "I'd never presume to control them."

Spydran gave what sounded like a contemptuous snort and took a couple of smooth steps backward, raising its massive clawed arms. Energy coursed through those arms and rippled around it. It called, and nanovor began to answer.

They popped into being around Spydran: the wasplike Circuit Flyer, two yellow and black armored Electroshields, as well as nanovor like the ones they had just faced: the Gamma Fury and the Phase Spiker. More popped up—two Battle Krakens—and Lucas found himself backing up until his back was to the crystal firewall. Drew appeared next to him.

"So. Think we can take it?" she asked conversationally, and he had never been so glad for her flippant manner.

"Uh. Thanks for not running off like they did. And I'm not sure."

Drew snorted. "I'm going to assume that the fact that you just compared me to the Snake Pit has to do with the considerable stress you're under. Dude, I told you I have your back."

"Someday you'll have to tell me how you beat both Ben and Bulk," he said and put out his own pool of energy. His nanovor had had time to resurrect and come back, hopefully a little stronger, and he called them. He gave his Storm Spinner an extra pat to thank it for the sacrifice it had made to get him and Dana out of the tunnel, then focused on Spydran.

A quick count of the twitching, buzzing, and lumbering

nanovor surrounding him showed that Spydran had been able to summon seven nanovor, which now waited at its feet.

"It doesn't have that many, not for a sensei. I wonder why?"

"It wasn't prepared, it thinks we'll be an easy target, it didn't eat its Wheaties—does it really matter?" Drew asked, testing her leashes on her rested nanovor.

"I almost believe we've got a chance, but we're still down six to seven. How did you beat Ben and Bulk?" Lucas asked as Spydran sent its first nanovor against them.

"No time to tell you. Follow my lead and you'll figure it out!" Drew said.

Drew sent out her nanovor, and Lucas decided to mirror her moves. Hers went out on the right, his on the left. Instead of meeting Spydran's nanovor in the middle, they flanked them, attacking from the side, first with ranged attacks, then with the Magnamods wading into battle. The less-armored nanovor let the Magnamods take on two or more attackers while they attacked from the rear using whatever ranged attacks they could.

It worked, to begin with. Drew's slow Tank Strider waded into battle, attracting the Gamma Fury and the Electroshield. As it took the beatings from those two, her Plasma Locust darted around the battlefield, blowing nanovor off their feet or jumping in to attack and leaping back out.

Lucas took his cue and sent his Plasma Lash in to meet up with the aggressive Phase Spiker and hopefully gain the attention of the green Spike Hornet, with its many tendrils stemming from its head. Spydran saw their plan soon enough, though, and sent the Spike Hornet to the perimeter, where the Storm Hunter was attacking with ranged attacks. It wrapped its tendrils around the Storm Hunter, and they began trading blows in close range. The Phase Spiker moved to join the Spike Hornet in the double-team action, but the Plasma Lash hit it from behind with a Head Whip, and Lucas whooped as the most aggressive nanovor on the field fell over, charred into a husk.

"That's great. Don't get cocky!" Drew shouted at him, managing her own nanovor. While she had been lucky in fighting Dana's, Ben's, and Bulk's nanovor, Spydran's were getting the best of her. Her plan to send her Tank Strider into the fray resulted in its messy destruction under the attacks of four nanovor, even as her Plasma Locust overcame the Gamma Fury, slicing its head from its shoulders.

Lucas was having an easier time, now facing two of Spydran's with his own two nanovor, the Storm Spinner and the Storm Hunter. Spydran's nanovor, the Spike Hornet and a Battle Kraken, both had tentacles that the Storm Spinner loved to target with its Spin Strike. One lucky hit and half the Battle Kraken's ropy black tentacles went flying. This reduced the 'vor's Tangle ability, giving Lucas the advantage. He set his Storm Hunter on the Spike Hornet and let the Storm Spinner finish off the Battle Kraken.

The Battle Kraken exploded in a flourish of green goo, and the Storm Spinner danced into the melee to help Drew. His Plasma Lash wasn't faring as well, getting hit hard by Spydran's other Battle Kraken and one of the Electroshields, but the Storm Spinner froze both enemy nanovor so the Plasma Lash could get free. They finished off both nanovor with ranged attacks, and Lucas raised his arm to his face to avoid the messy result of the fight.

Lucas's Storm Hunter fell to the attack of the Spike Hornet, but the Plasma Lash was strong enough for another Head Whip, which finished off the Spike Hornet.

That left the final Electroshield, which Drew's Plasma Locust took perhaps too much glee in dissecting in front of her.

Their remaining nanovor turned their focus to Spydran, who took a slow step backward.

"You were saying, Spydran? Got anything else you need to let us know?" Lucas asked.

"Humans," the sensei spat. "Our next encounter will have a different outcome."

It winked out before the nanovor could attack, and Lucas and Drew looked at each other.

"Did we win?" asked Drew.

"I think we did," said Lucas.

"I suppose we don't get to enjoy it, do we?" she asked.

Lucas shook his head. "We've got to go stop whatever Dana's up to. She can still mess things up big time for me and Madame Zeldara, if the contest is still rigged in my favor. She could expose me or do any number of things."

"True, but savor this moment, Lucas, what we did, I mean. We won. We beat Spydran," Drew grinned at him. "That's worth at least an ice-cream sundae later."

"You're absolutely right," said Lucas.

Lucas and Drew linked hands and together winked out of the nanosphere.

Dana had failed at getting her father back into his job. She had failed in a nanovor battle with those freshmen. And she'd failed in manipulating the nanosphere to her liking.

There was one person to blame. And Dana knew just where to find him.

She stormed out of the empty classroom and down the hall. Ben and Bulk stood outside the senior English classroom and stared at the floor as Principal Sturn berated them, Ben covered in caramel and Bulk sporting a large lump on his forehead.

"Bullying, destruction of private property, disrupting our science fair in front of a local reporter! Boys, I really don't know where to begin." As Dana walked past them without meeting their eyes, the principal put her hands on her hips. "No. I think we'll begin with three days' suspension, then two weeks of detention. You'll write a letter of apology to every person whose experiment you destroyed and then . . ."

Dana was finally out of earshot. Ben and Bulk had been punished before and it hadn't hurt them then. Her father would be annoyed that Ben wouldn't be around to help him, but he'd probably be annoyed by much more than that before the day was done.

Her anger bubbled up fresh again, and she pushed the gymnasium doors with both hands, forcing them to fly open.

The science fair was in a shambles. Some students were in tears, others were furious. A disgruntled janitor was heading to clean up the spilled caramel, and some students were bravely trying to reassemble their projects.

Nathan wore Lucas's nametag and was showing some parents the mysteries of Madame Zeldara when Dana came storming up to him.

"Uh, excuse me," he said, as Dana pulled him away from the booth.

"BEWARE!" shouted Madame Zeldara after them.

"Did you tell Lucas and Drew what I had planned? Did

you ruin everything?"

Nathan glared at her. "Really, Dana. You didn't think Lucas would figure out why his project was malfunctioning?"

"I can't help but think you helped them out," she said, looking past him to the fortune-teller yelling BEWARE.

"Of course I helped them out. They're my friends. But I didn't tell them what was done, and I didn't tell them who did it. But if you want to keep talking about it, here they come."

Dana didn't turn around to look. She pulled at the PAR-TICIPANT badge around his neck. "This isn't over, Nathan. Not by a long shot."

She stomped away from him, looking around for her father. She had some bad news to deliver.

Drew snickered as Dana scuttled away from their booth as they approached.

Lucas grinned. "We are pretty awesome, aren't we?"

"We're the Battle Mastahs, Lucas. Don't you forget that."

They bumped fists, then greeted Nathan. He looked nervous. "Did everything go okay?"

"Yeah. Dana tried to upload some information into S.K.Y. Labs' databases," Lucas said. "We stopped her."

Drew snorted. "That's putting it mildly. You didn't tell

him about the nanovor battle, or Spydran, or the epic battle where I proved myself—"

Lucas stopped her arms from waving madly and said, "Yeah, we can hit those details later, Drew. We have stuff we need to do. How did it go on your end, Nathan?"

"I had fun playing the carnie," he said. He made his voice more nasal and puffed his chest out, " 'Step right up! Everyone's a winner! Something for the little lady, perhaps?' People ate it up. But when teachers came by, I just turned the nametag around and said that you were in the bathroom and I was watching your booth."

"Did, uh, anything, you know, bad happen?" Lucas asked.

"No terrible secrets were revealed, if that's what you're worried about."

Lucas sighed and relaxed. "And you removed whatever was plugged into Madame Zeldara."

Nathan rummaged around in his backpack, sitting beside Madame Zeldara. He pulled out a dongle with a familiar-looking touch screen phone attached. He waved it at them, and Lucas took it. "Man. I saw her fiddling with this. I had no idea."

Nearly dropping the phone as he remembered what Dana

had told him, Lucas said, "Wait, we have to find Doc Zap! The Diamondbacks are going to make sure I win. Doc should be here by now. He'll be able to stop Diamondback!"

Nathan put his hand on Lucas's shoulder. "Calm down, dude. Doc Zap showed up while you two were gone. I told him what I know—that the Snake Pit is up to something, probably having to do with the recording of data from Madame Zeldara. He figured it out from there. He's a smart guy, that Doc Zap."

"Oh, man. Really? That's great news!" Lucas collapsed into a chair.

"Also," Nathan said, "the teachers are looking for Ben and Bulk to hold them accountable for the destruction of no less than seven science projects."

"Oh, thank goodness!" Drew said, plopping down on the floor beside Lucas's chair.

"Uh, Lucas?" Nathan held out Lucas's badge. "Do you mind being you again? It's tiring, honestly."

Lucas laughed. "Tell me about it."

The students gathered at the foot of the stage in the gymnasium while the judges conferred one last time. Lucas, Nathan, and Drew stood together in the front.

"You glad you did the right thing?" Drew asked him.

Lucas sighed and looked down at his feet. "Yeah, I guess so."

"Look at it this way. If you win now, you'll know you were the best. If you had won before, you'd never know."

"And I'd lose the great gift of your company, since you'd be so annoyed with you me you wouldn't talk to me anymore," Lucas said, grinning at her.

"Well. Maybe," Drew said. "We'll never know, will we?"

Nathan shushed them as Doc Zap took the microphone.

"Thanks, everyone, for coming to the Emerald City Science Fair! I've noted everyone here who will get the extra credit on your science scores, but we will be talking in class about the different projects—what worked, what didn't."

Some groans came up from the audience, but Doc Zap raised his eyebrow and they subsided. "We regret the, uh, excitement that happened today. We would like to assure you that the judges had already graded all of the projects beforehand, so the current state of the projects will not affect the scores."

More grumbles came up from the audience, and Doc Zap held his hands up to stifle them. "Here to list the honorable mentions, let's welcome Dr. Hatch from S.K.Y. Lab

Technologies! These winners will go to the state science fair next weekend, as well as receive medals," he said, holding the medals up.

Dr. Hatch came up to the microphone, smiling. "It's certainly been an interesting day, and we are looking forward to seeing these fine young minds develop. The first honorable mention will go to Jennifer Greer for her Rube Goldberg caramel-apple machine!"

The girl came on the stage to applause, took the medal from Doc Zap, and stood beside him.

Dr. Hatch approached the microphone again. "Let's give her a big hand, shall we?" The group broke into applause again, Nathan clapping extra loudly.

Lucas felt good about the fact that the poor girl had won something since her machine had been destroyed during his adventures. The second and third honorable mentions went to the boy who did the hydroponic-corn experiment and, surprisingly, the girl who did the scale model of the solar system.

"If they're going to state, we need to help them fix up their experiments," Drew whispered. "It's only fair. They shouldn't lose because Ben and Bulk busted their stuff up while they were chasing us."

"You're right," Lucas said, feeling lighter.

Dr. Hatch waited for all the applause for the honorable-mention winners to die down. She smiled widely. "And now we have the grand-prize winner, who will win a medal, an interview for a summer internship at S.K.Y. Lab Technologies, and the opportunity to go to the state science fair next weekend!"

Drew grabbed his arm in anticipation, and Lucas tried to remember to breathe. After all they'd been through, he needed a regular, everyday victory.

"And the grand-prize winner of the Emerald City Science Fair is Lucas Nelson, with the project of Madame Zeldara, the Fortune-Teller!"

Lucas had to have Nathan help him remove Drew, who was hugging him fiercely, so he could approach the stage. Grinning widely, he climbed the stairs and approached Dr. Hatch, the S.K.Y. Lab Technologies scientists, and Doc Zap, who finally smiled at him.

Madame Zeldara had never predicted this.

"Vegetarian, meat lover's, or cheese?" Nathan asked Drew.

"Gee, all of the extremes, no middle," she said. "Vegetarian, I guess."

Lucas decided not to play favorites and got one slice of each, though he nearly choked on the meat lover's. They sat in Doc Zap's classroom, chowing down on Doc's congratulatory feast, three pizzas for the four of them.

"I felt it was prudent to choose three pizzas from the different extremes," Doc Zap said. "I didn't know what people liked. You are, of course, welcome."

Drew colored and gave Doc her thousand-watt smile. "And we do appreciate it, Doc, truly!"

"So what happened while we were stopping Dana, Doc?" asked Lucas.

"It was really interesting, actually," Doc Zap said. "After I arrived at the booth, Nathan told me that something fishy was going on. I knew to look for Dr. Diamondback, so I alerted the head judge, an old friend from the university, that something might be going with the electronic clipboards. He recalled all of them and said they had a defect. He found some evidence of tampering, especially since Lucas had the same score out of 100 by each judge."

"That's kinda the stupidest thing I've ever heard," Lucas said. "I mean, did he not think anyone would notice?"

"Well if no one had been watching for it, they probably wouldn't have," Doc Zap said, snagging another cheese piece for himself and settling back in his chair. "The scores were tallied, so we would have gotten just one number. Anyway, he told everyone the clipboards had malfunctioned and required judges to hand in physical copies of scores."

"Old-school judging!" said Lucas.

"And it turns out you won anyway, but at least now we know for sure," Doc Zap said.

Drew gave Lucas a meaningful look, and he made a face at her.

"Drew, you and Nathan will need to go with Lucas to the state competition to make sure the Snake Pit doesn't try to hack Madame Zeldara again. Are you going to be able to do that?" Doc Zap asked.

"Of course," Drew said immediately.

"I'll have to check my schedule," Nathan mumbled through a mouthful of pizza.

"Good. Well, we can relax for the moment, as Dr. Diamondback has been stopped for now. And now he has two disgraces to bounce back from. Yes, you guys had a full day."

Lucas glanced at Drew, then back at Doc Zap. "The Diamondbacks aren't our biggest problem, Doc. After we stopped Dana in the nanosphere, we ran into Spydran."

Doc Zap stopped chewing. He leaned forward. "I'm listening."

Lucas nodded. "It summoned a swarm and attacked me. But it wasn't a very big swarm, and I got out of it okay."

"Hello?" Drew yelled, punching him. "YOU got out of it? YOU beat Spydran? Did you forget that someone else was there?"

Lucas grinned. "Oh yeah, my nanovor were there. You should have seen my Storm Hunter, Doc. He was a real hero!"

Drew launched herself at him, but Nathan caught the back of her pants, and she struggled, reaching for Lucas desperately. "You're a dead man, Nelson!" she said.

Lucas grinned and didn't look at her, focusing entirely on Doc Zap. "Oh, and I think my Storm Spinner actually sacrificed himself to let me and Dana get through the firewall, all on his own! I was amazed at how much he helped me!"

"Lucas!" she yelled and struggled more against Nathan.

"It was a tough battle to do on my own, but I managed to

make it out somehow. Only no one will ever know exactly what happened, as there was no one else there to tell the tale."

Nathan let Drew go at that point, and she darted forward, her fingers extended, aiming for Lucas's ribs.

His last thoughts before Drew descended upon him were that he would always be able to defeat anyone as long as these friends were by his side.

After the Science Fair

From "Everywhere Fast," Lucas Nelson's Journal

So yeah, Saturday was the science fair, the introduction of Madame Zeldara to the world, and the most exciting battle I've ever had in the nanosphere—and I won the science fair. Oh, and I saw Doc Zap actually smile.

Not much happened on Sunday.

So now I'm getting ready for the state show on Saturday. I'll be working to make Madame Zeldara more secure. If I have time, I think I'll give her some keywords to avoid so we don't embarrass any of the subjects. Yeah. That's a good idea.

I'm glad Drew is coming with me to state. I never know what the Snake Pit is going to be up to, and she's always got my back. She wants to protect me from Dana. I don't think Dana is so bad. I just think she's a little obsessed with getting her dad back in a big-time science job. And who doesn't want their dad to work?

I just wish she had a more constructive way to get him his old job back.

But Spydran worries me. It should have been able to summon a lot more nanovor. What weakened it? I want to know what it wants—beyond the end of all humans, that is. I'm afraid some day it's going to get ugly, and only people who are familiar with nanovor will be able to stop it.

This, of course, is why we need more kids to join the Lab Rats and learn how to train and battle nanovor. The more people we have controlling nanovor, the less chance Spydran has to take over. So if you know anyone who shows a good mind for strategy, an interest in electronics, and a keen desire to save the world, lemme know.

And, hey, if you found the code I mentioned in this book, you might be one of the ones who can help! Just plug in the code at the front of the book and send it to me at:

www.hanoverhigh.com/hacked

~Lucas Out